Macy Goes to the Lake

Love Queen
LET YOUR LOVE SHINE THROUGH

Written and Illustrated by:
Christine Kuschewki

This book is dedicated to my siblings. Kathy, Sue, Mary and Jim, thank you for your love and support in all I do. I am so grateful to have each of you as my lifelong best friends!

Love Queen

LET YOUR LOVE SHINE THROUGH

Macy is going to the lake today. She is so excited to swim and have fun. Macy is riding in the truck with mom and her friend.

On the way to the lake, they see some burros on the side of the road. Look at the mama burro and her baby!

They finally arrive and Macy gets on to the boat. She is happy. Just look at that smile! Macy loves to go with her mom, and the lake is one of her favortie places.

The boat goes fast across the water. Macy lays down for the ride and let's the wind blow through her fur.

Mom puts on Macy's life jacket so she stays safe in the water. Macy is ready to go for a swim. Do you think the water is cold?

Look at Macy go! The water is cool and refreshing. Macy swims and swims. She is having a great time!

Macy jumps up onto the big orange float! She rests a little bit and enjoys the sunshine. Macy likes the big orange float because she can be close to mom.

Look at Macy! She is riding on the jet ski with mom. Macy thinks this is fun. Mom doesn't go too fast so they stay safe. The wind blows Macy's ears and the water splashes in her face. Macy smiles!

Time for a break. Swimming is hard work. Macy wraps up in a towel to dry off and stay warm.

Macy watches the kids swim. They are splashing and laughing. Macy just watches from the boat. Everyone is having a great time at the lake!

Macy is hungry. She has a snack. Mom gives her a sausage and some cheese. Macy gets a drink of water too.

Macy wants to drive the boat. She jumps up into the driver's seat and gets ready to drive.

Mom tells Macy she cannot drive. Macy is sad, but gets down. She goes back to watching the kids. They are riding jet skis and swimming. Macy loves to watch the kids.

What's that?! Macy sees the littlest boy blow bubbles. She tries to catch the bubbles. Macy tells him to do it again. She likes to pop bubbles.

Some ducks come by the boat to see if they can join the fun. They quack and mom throws them a treat. They gobble it up and quack for more.

Macy lays in the sun and takes a nap. She enjoys the warmth of the sun while sleeping.

Mom tells Macy to wake up to look at the beautiful rainbow. Macy opens her eyes to look. She thinks it is pretty too.

The sun is starting to set, which means it is time to go home. Macy is sad to leave the lake, but she is tired and is ready to go home to sleep in her comfy bed.

Macy gets into the truck for the ride home, She says good-bye to the lake. She can't wait to come back to swim again soon!

Macy and her mom went to Lake Pleasant in Peoria, Arizona.

Macy's Candid Shots

Christine Kuschewski has been a special education teacher for 22 years. She loves teaching children how to read. Her love for books and education has led her to writing children's books.

Christine and Macy live in Arizona. Macy loves to spend time with her best friends, Toby, Kona and their family. Macy is a 7 year-old Bichon Frise, Poodle, Maltese and Shih-Tzu mix. Everyone who meets Macy falls in love with her. Together Christine and Macy enjoy spreading love to the world.

Love Queen
LET YOUR LOVE SHINE THROUGH

Macy's World Titles

Made in the USA
Columbia, SC
23 November 2022

71462415R00027